Primrose

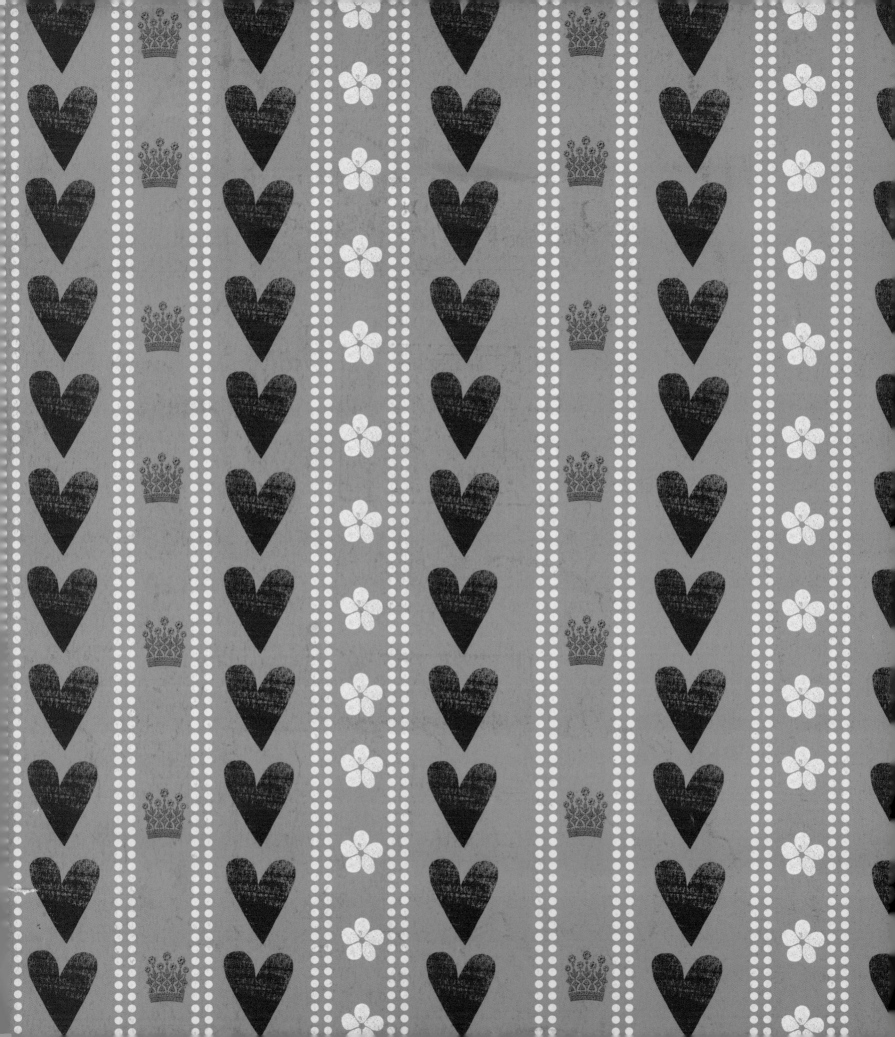

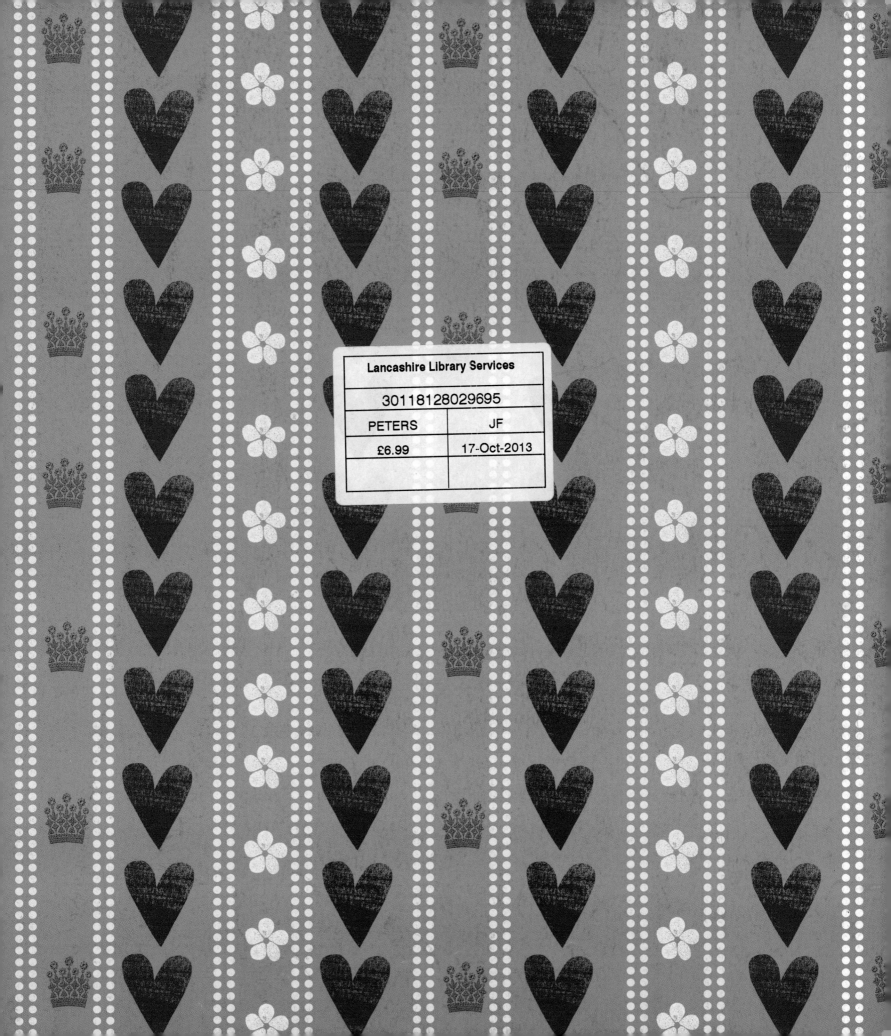

For HRH Siân Smith
(my lovely little mum!)
A.T.S.

x

This book has been borrowed from

The Royal Library

Published by
Scholastic Children's Books
Providers of Royal Stories to
HRH Princess Primrose &
HRH Percy

First published in 2013 by Scholastic Children's Books
Euston House, 24 Eversholt Street
London NW1 1DB
a division of Scholastic Ltd
www.scholastic.co.uk
London ~ New York ~ Toronto ~ Sydney ~ Auckland
Mexico City ~ New Delhi ~ Hong Kong

Text and Illustrations copyright © 2013 Alex T. Smith
HB ISBN 978 1407 10965 7
PB ISBN 978 1407 10966 4
Printed in Singapore

1 3 5 7 9 10 8 6 4 2

Primrose

Alex T. Smith

TOOT! TOOT!

SCHOLASTIC

Once upon a time in a pretty pink palace, there lived a pretty pink princess called Primrose.

She had a pretty pink tiara, two prancing pink ponies and a plump little pug named Percy.

But Princess Primrose wasn't happy. The trouble was that life at the palace was boring, boring, boring.

Everyone was terribly serious and properly proper, and Primrose longed to have some fun.

The King rolled his eyes when he caught Primrose climbing trees in the Royal Orchard.

"Primrose!" he hollered, "Princesses don't hang upside down! They sit neatly beneath trees on a chair and do their princess homework!"

And the King made
Primrose pull up a chair
and learn how to wave
politely when travelling
in the Royal Carriage.

Primrose's mother, the Queen, gave a loud shriek when she found Primrose and Percy playing dressing up in their bedroom.

"Primrose!" she gasped, "Princesses don't monkey about!"

And the Queen made Primrose and Percy
change out of their silly clothes and into
more suitable and **very uncomfortable**
royal outfits.

(Percy secretly quite liked his suit!)

It was the same everywhere Primrose turned.
"Princesses **don't** play boardgames!" moaned the maids.

"Princesses **don't** dig up muddy vegetables!" grumbled the gardener.

And when Primrose asked to help bake some cupcakes in the Royal Kitchen, the cook almost fainted.

"Princesses don't dabble with dough!" he hissed nervously. "They would get their hands messy and drop egg on their dresses!"

And he shoo-shoo-shooed her quickly out of the kitchen.

"Something **must** be done about Primrose," sighed the Queen one day. "She simply can't carry on like this. She is a princess after all and she must learn to behave like one."

Everybody agreed.
There was only one thing for it.
Somebody must call
Grandmama.

If anybody could turn Primrose
into a proper princess it was
Her Royal Highness.

Royal Decree
In extreme
emergencies,
telephone
Grandmama
immediately!

When Grandmama arrived…

...everyone
was on their very
best behaviour.

Everyone apart
from Primrose.
She just carried
on as normal.

"I see exactly what
the problem is here!"
tutted Grandmama.

"What?" asked the King and Queen together.

"I'm not going to tell you," Grandmama boomed in her bossiest voice, "but you will all do exactly as I say."

The King and Queen nodded nervously.

First, Grandmama ordered the King to climb a tree in the Royal Orchard.

The King was shocked to begin with, but Grandmama waggled a finger at him and he clambered **all** the way to the top.

"Gosh!" the King panted, "I didn't even remember we had a Royal Treehouse... Well, this is fun!" And he and Primrose had a nice cup of tea and a giggle in the leaves.

Next, Grandmama ordered the
Queen to change her clothes.

"Golly!" cried the Queen.
"This is fun!" and she bounced
on the bed and laughed and
laughed and laughed.

The rest of the day passed busily for the Royal Family.

They spent the afternoon playing snakes and ladders…

…digging up muddy vegetables…

PULL!

...and baking treats for tea, making a **marvellous mess** in the kitchen.

"You see," smiled Grandmama at the end of the day, "it doesn't do anybody any good being so serious all the time. What this place needed was a sprinkle of fun and some good old belly-laughs."

Everyone agreed that Grandmama was right – as always.

"Now," said Grandmama, giving Primrose
a big cuddle, "I really must be going."

"Would you like to borrow
the Royal Carriage?"
asked Primrose politely.

"Oh no, thank you darling,"
chuckled Grandmama,
"I have a **much** better
way of travelling…"

"I might be a Royal Highness,
but Grannies...
like having fun too!

Cheerio my dears!"

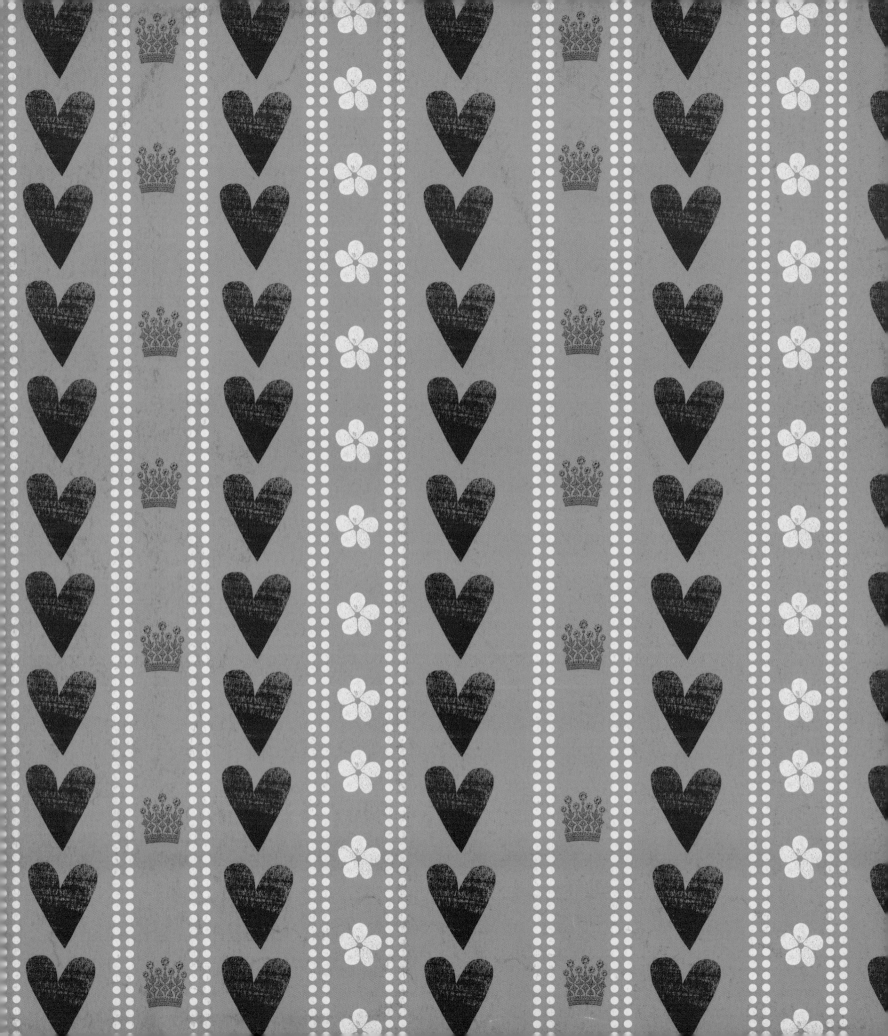

The End